ILLUSTRATED BY

JULIA DONALDSON ★ LYDIA MONKS

WHAT THE LADYBUG HEARD NEXT

Henry Holt and Company · New York

There once was a ladybug, shy and small.
She lived on a farm and looked after it all:

The cow in her shed, the horse in his stall,
The cats who purred on the garden wall,
The barn full of straw, the field full of sheep,
The kennel where the dog lay fast asleep,
The fish in the pond, the drake and the duck,
The hive of bees and the heap of muck,
The hog in his sty, the goose in her pen,
And the coop, which was home to the fat red hen.

Now the fat red hen with her thin brown legs
Laid lots and lots of speckled eggs.
But then—oh help, oh no, oh dear—
Those eggs began to disappear.
Each morning all the eggs had gone.
And the animals asked, "What's going on?"

Then the ladybug said, "Leave it to me.
I'll hear what I hear and I'll see what I see."

She saw two men in a big, black van
With a light and a sack and a cunning plan.
(They were Hefty Hugh and Lanky Len,
Who had been to jail but were out again.)
Said Lanky Len to Hefty Hugh, "Let's steal another egg or two."

But Hefty Hugh said, "Listen, Len—
I vote we steal the fat red hen.
We'll make our way to the chicken coop
And scoop her up in one fell swoop.
Just think of all those eggs she'll lay us,
And all the money folks will pay us!"

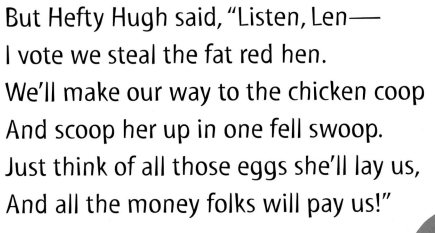

And Len replied, "We'll soon be rich.
It makes my fingers start to itch."

The ladybug, filled with great alarm,
Told the animals on the farm,
"Hefty Hugh and Lanky Len
Are planning to steal the fat red hen!"

Then the cow said, "Moo!" and the hen said, "Cluck!"
"Hiss!" said the goose. "Quack!" said the duck.
"Neigh!" said the horse. "Oink!" said the hog.
"Baa!" said the sheep and "Woof!" said the dog.

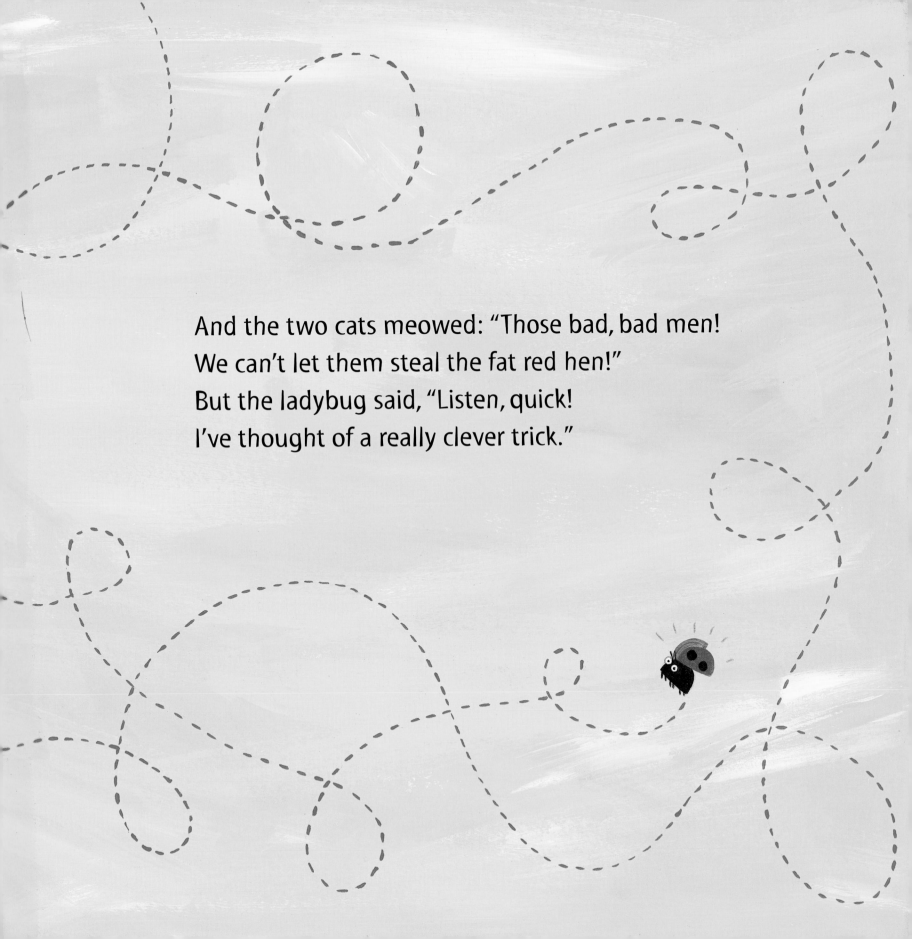

And the two cats meowed: "Those bad, bad men!
We can't let them steal the fat red hen!"
But the ladybug said, "Listen, quick!
I've thought of a really clever trick."

In the dead of night, the two bad men
Opened the coop and snatched the hen.
But the fat red hen began to cluck,
"Why don't you steal the downy duck?

She lays much bigger eggs than mine
And people say they taste divine."

"Good thinking, hen," said Lanky Len.
They tiptoed to the pond, but then . . .

The downy duck began to quack,
"Oh please don't put me in your sack.
Why don't you steal the goose instead?
She's bigger still, and better fed.
Her eggs are huge, and tasty, too."
"Good thinking, duck," said Hefty Hugh.

But when they tried to seize the goose,
She hissed at them, "I'm not much use.
Why don't you steal that great big bird,
The super-duper Snuggly Snerd?"

"What?" said Len, and "Who?" said Hugh.
The goose replied, "I thought you knew.
She lays the biggest eggs of all.
Each one looks like a basketball."

The duck joined in: "She's friendly, too.
I'm sure she'd love to live with you.
She'll put an end to all your cares.
You'll very soon be millionaires."
"Where is this Snerd?" asked Lanky Len.
"Not far away," chimed in the hen.
"She lives inside that big brown heap.
You'll find her there. She's fast asleep."

The two thieves laughed. "We've got it made!
Let's take turns with the farmer's spade."
They dug and they dug, and Len said, "Pooh,
It stinks!" and Hugh said, "So do you."

And Len said, "Where's that giant bird,
The super-duper Snuggly Snerd?"
"She's rather shy," the goose replied.
"She must be hiding deep inside."

So they dug a tunnel, nice and deep.
"That's it!" said Hugh. "Now, in we creep."

"I think we're nearly there," said Len.
"The Snerd will soon be ours!" But then . . .

The heap collapsed, and Hugh said, "Yuck!
We're covered head to toe in muck."

And Len complained, "There *is* no Snerd.
They just made up that giant bird."

Then the other animals gathered round
And all let out a deafening sound.

NEIGH!

MOO!

OINK!

BAA!

WOOF WOOF!

MEOW!

What a racket! What a row!

The farmer woke and said, "Goodness me!"
And he had a word with his prize Queen Bee.

And the bees chased after the two bad men,
Who never came back to the farm again!

Then the cow said, "Moo!" and the hen said, "Cluck!"
"Hiss!" said the goose. "Quack!" said the duck.
"Neigh!" said the horse. "Oink!" said the hog.
"Baa!" said the sheep and "Woof!" said the dog.
And the farmer cheered, and both cats purred,

But the ladybug never said a word . . .
And neither did the Snuggly Snerd.

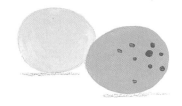

For Vincent —J. D.

For Ava and Scarlett —L. M.

Henry Holt and Company, *Publishers since 1866*
Henry Holt® is a registered trademark of Macmillan Publishing Group, LLC
175 Fifth Avenue, New York, NY 10010 • mackids.com

Library of Congress Cataloging-in-Publication Data
Names: Donaldson, Julia, author. | Monks, Lydia, illustrator.
Title: What the ladybug heard next / Julia Donaldson ; illustrated by Lydia Monks.
Description: New York : Henry Holt and Company, 2018. | Sequel to: What the ladybug heard. | Originally published in the United Kingdom in 2015 by Macmillan Children's books.
Summary: When Hefty Hugh and Lanky Len return to the farm hoping to steal the fat red hen, the little spotty ladybug enlists the other animals to stop them.
Identifiers: LCCN 2017021148 | ISBN 9781250156525 (hardcover)
Subjects: | CYAC: Stories in rhyme. | Ladybugs—Fiction. | Domestic animals—Fiction. | Animal sounds—Fiction. | Robbers and outlaws—Fiction.
Classification: LCC PZ8.3.D7235 Whk 2018 | DDC [E]—dc2e
LC record available at https://lccn.loc.gov/2017021148

Our books may be purchased in bulk for promotional, educational, or business use. Please contact your local bookseller or the
Macmillan Corporate and Premium Sales Department at (800) 221-7945 ext. 5442 or by e-mail at MacmillanSpecialMarkets@macmillan.com.

Originally published in the United Kingdom in 2015 by Macmillan Children's Books
First American edition, 2018
Printed in China by WKT Co. Ltd., Shenzhen, Guangdong Province

1 3 5 7 9 10 8 6 4 2